This Book Belongs to

....

For information address Disney Press, 1101 Flower Street, Glendale, California 91201.

ISBN 978-1-4847-9950-5

FAC-038091-17174

Printed in the United States of America

Library of Congress Control Number: 2016938193

First Hardcover Edition, August 2017

1 3 5 7 9 10 8 6 4 2

For more Disney Press fun, visit www.disneybooks.com

Logo Applies to Text Stock Only

Dinglehoppers and Thingamabobs

By **Livingstone Crouse**

Illustrated by **Amy Mebberson**

LOS ANGELES • NEW YORK

Ahoy, there!

Seagull coming in for a–

OOOF!

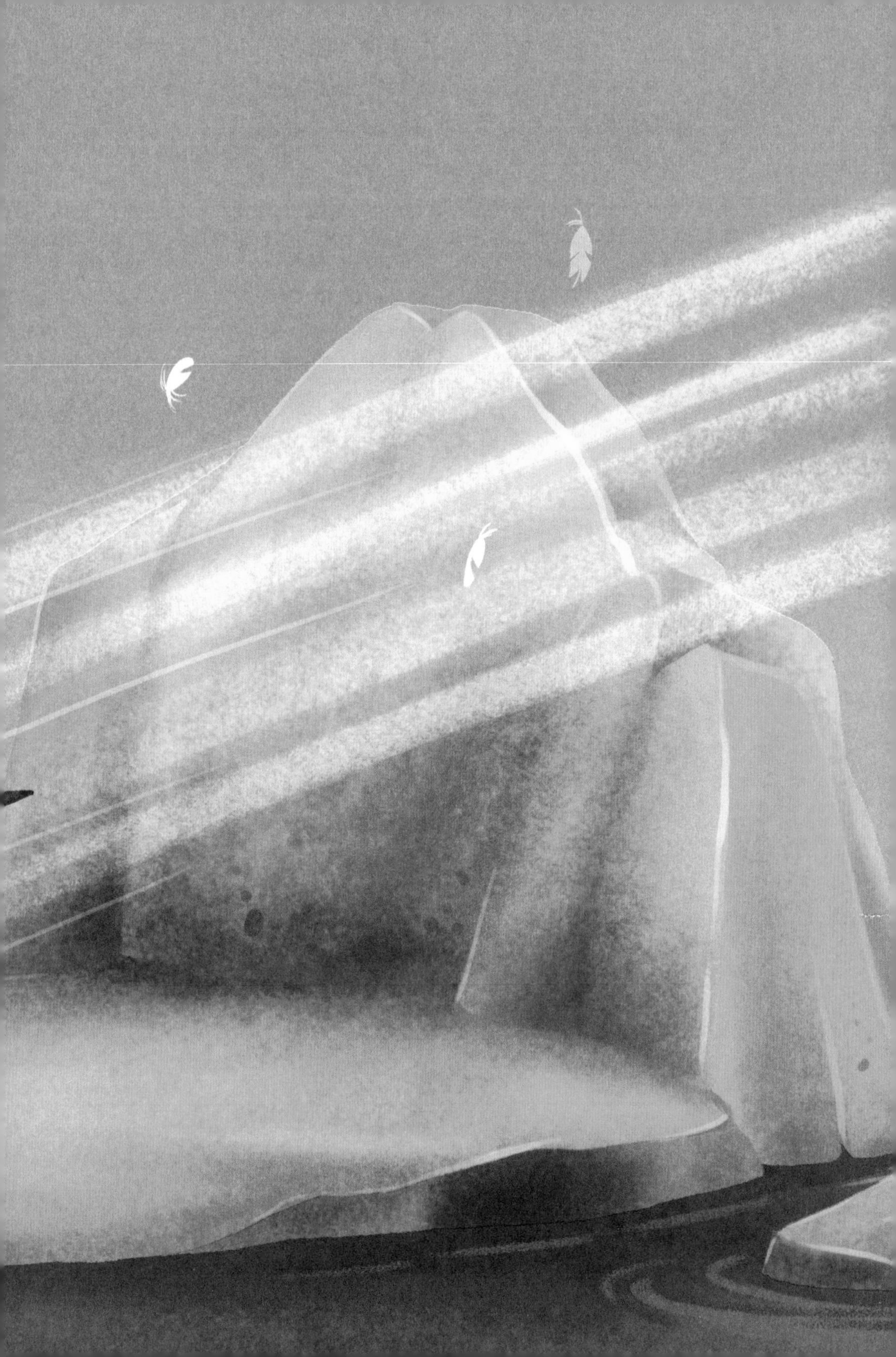

—landing.

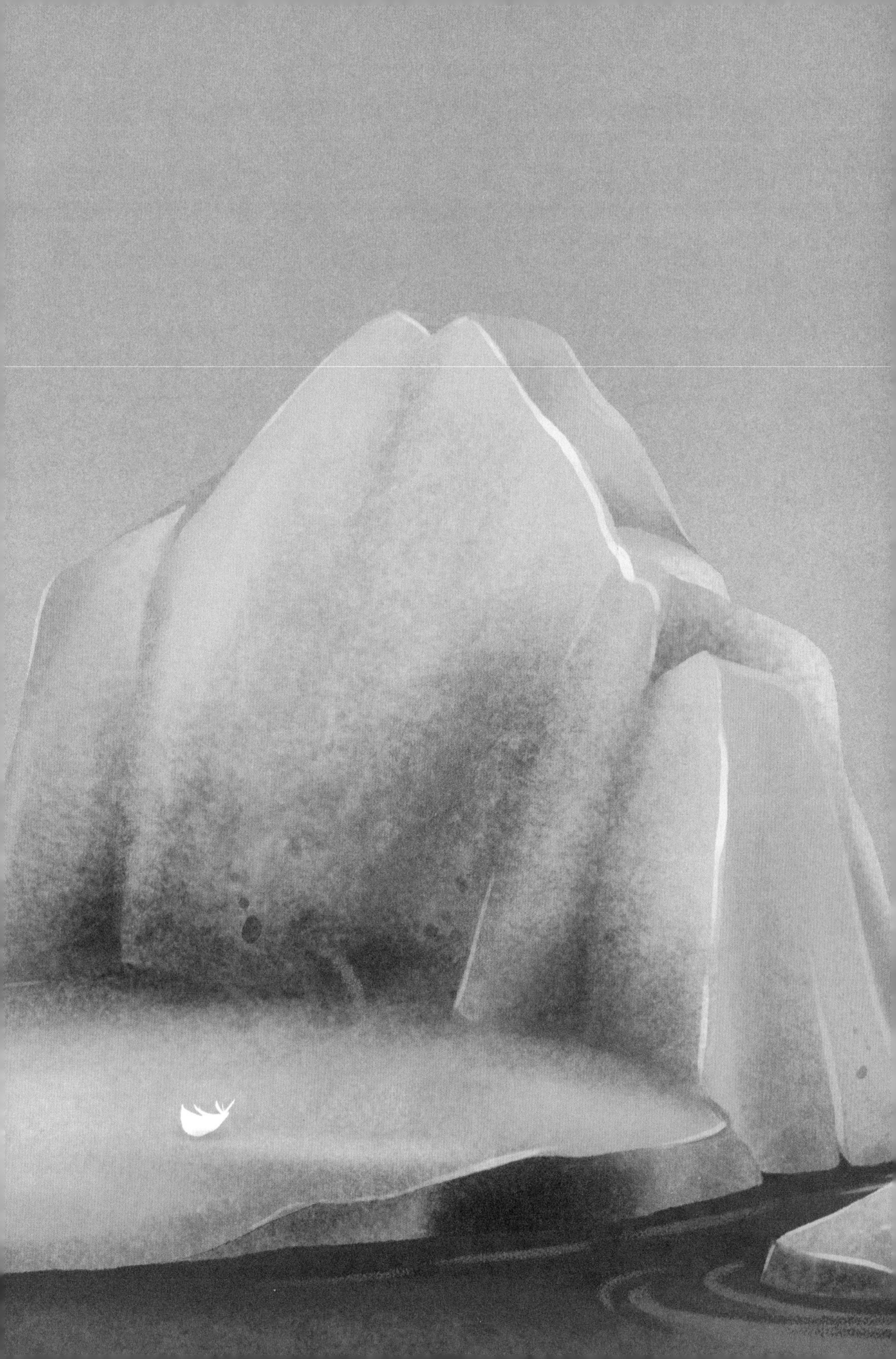

Oh, hey, kid!

Thought I had this rock to myself!

Well, as long as you're here, want to see my collection?

This . . .

is a

hiffenjugger!

Humans pile these babies up to see over rocks.

Land ho!

Aha!

The snarfblatt.

Invented to make music on quiet nights.

Hmmm.

Doesn't work.

Now this one . . .

the pookentick.

Used for spinning in **circles!**

Whoa!

Hey, kid! Wanna go?

What's that? My hair?

Nice, isn't it?

Batten my hatches, I've been

ruffled!!!

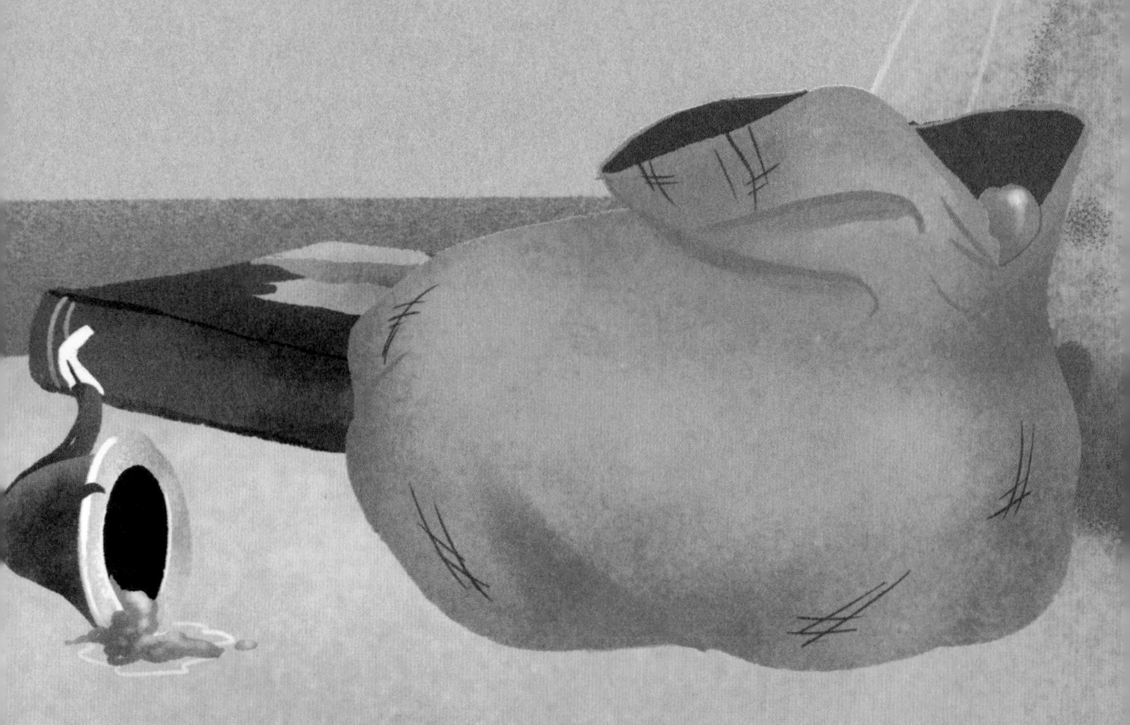

Hang on, kid.
I can fix this.

I just need . . .

No, not that.

I know there's one around
here somewhere.

Thar she blows!

Aha!

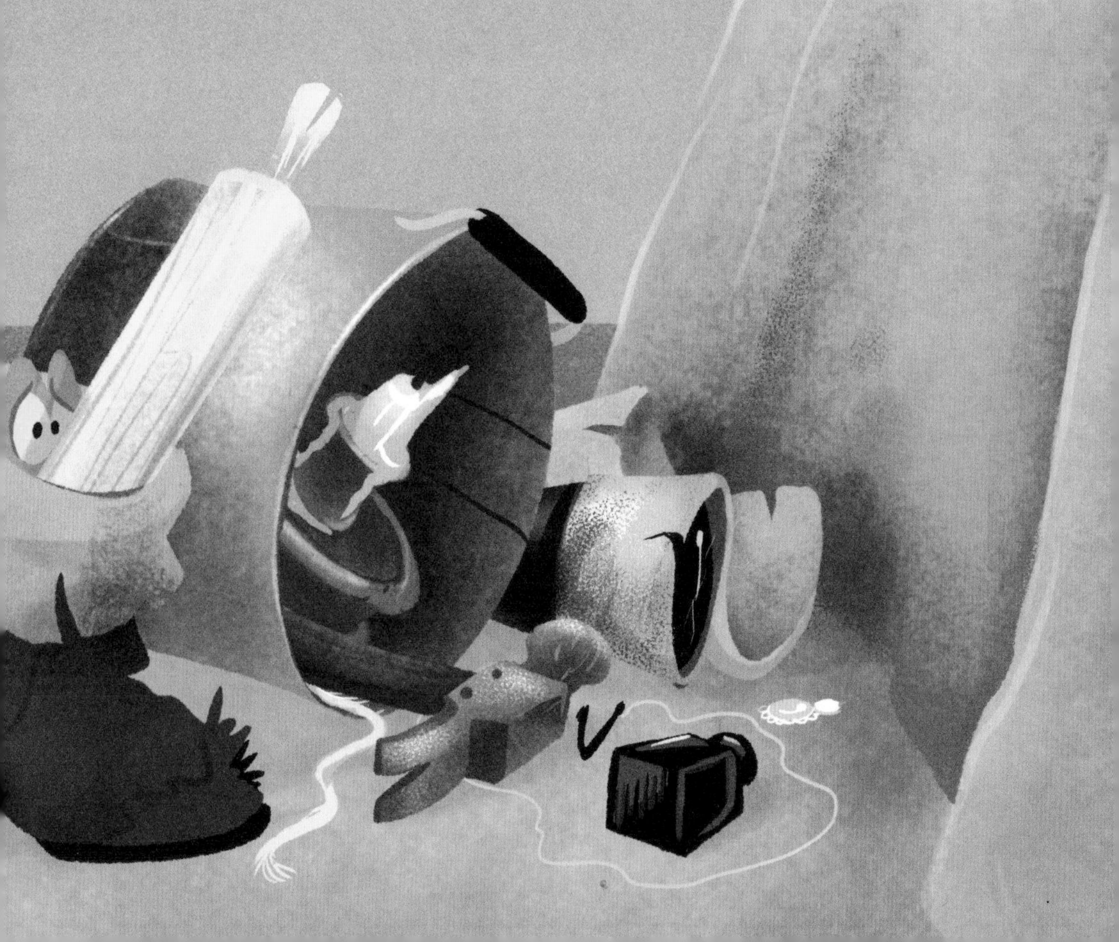

A DINGLEHOPPER!

A twirl here.
A yank there.
And . . .

…voilà!

An aesthetically pleasing
configuration of hair!

No good?

Still ruffled?

Never fear.
I've got just the
thing!

This

thingamabob

is perfect for
unruffling feathers,
don’tcha know.

Wrap this here.
Tuck that there.

MAYDAY!

MAYDAY!

Okay, there we go.
A quick tug and . . .

Still
ruffled?

You don't say.

I'm **sure** this

luggaloop

will work!

hmnm
hmm

Still
ruffled?

This calls for drastic measures.

Time for the

toppenbugle!

UMPH.

Mrflmfl.

Mrflmfl.

MUMMM...

Whew!

Now that we've got that out of the way, I have a question for you.

Do you happen
to know what
this
doohickey
is?